To Sam, Charissa, and our families,
who make us happy

Groundwood Books / House of Anansi Press
groundwoodbooks.com

We gratefully acknowledge for their financial support of our
publishing program the Canada Council for the Arts, the
Ontario Arts Council and the Government of Canada.

 Canada Council   Conseil des Arts
for the Arts   du Canada

 ONTARIO ARTS COUNCIL
CONSEIL DES ARTS DE L'ONTARIO
an Ontario government agency
un organisme du gouvernement de l'Ontario

With the participation of the Government of Canada
Avec la participation du gouvernement du Canada | Canadä

Library and Archives Canada Cataloguing in Publication
Tamaki, Mariko
Skim / by Mariko Tamaki and Jillian Tamaki.
ISBN 978-0-88899-964-1
I. Tamaki, Jillian II. Title.
PN6733.T34S55 2010   741.5'971   C2009-906513-4

Groundwood Books is committed to protecting our natural
environment. As part of our efforts, the interior of this book is
printed on paper from responsible sources.

Printed and bound in Canada

 MIX
Paper from
responsible sources
FSC® C016245
FSC
www.fsc.org

SKIM

Mariko Tamaki
AND **Jillian Tamaki**

g GROUNDWOOD BOOKS
HOUSE OF ANANSI PRESS
TORONTO   BERKELEY

Dear Diary,

Today Lisa said,
"Everyone thinks they are unique."

That is not unique!!

Part I

Fall

I am: Kimberly Keiko Cameron (aka Skim)

My best friend: Lisa Soor

My cat: Sumo ♡

Interests: Wicca, tarot cards, astrology
(me = Aquarius = very unpredictable), philosophy

Favorite color: ~~black~~ red

Year: 1993

Up until four last night, trying to take pictures of cast.

Decided it is impossible to take pictures of your right arm when you're right-handed.

(Duh.)

Would have gotten black cast, but had to get regular white instead.

Decided stitches are definitely cooler than broken bones.

Should have fallen on beer bottle.

Hey, Skim, what happened?

I broke my arm.

8

My mom says the heart attacks have turned my father into a cream puff.

My dad says my mother is a cold cynical woman who has no appreciation for a broken heart.

Mom says there's no way Dad's heart is broken.

Even if your father, who is an ASSHOLE, had a heart, it couldn't be broken. Your heart is a muscle.

My parents = serious issues.

My dad signed my cast with an ugly happy face that I am scratching off.

Me = serious issues.

IN OTHER NEWS!!!

Katie Matthews' boyfriend, John Reddear, who goes to
St. George's, dumped her. LE BIG DUMP! So this week
Katie is wearing big black hearts on her hands. She
draws them on with a sharpie in math class. Left
one is nicer than right one. Similar problem as cast
and photo.

It's kind of brutal watching someone walk around
with broken hearts on their hands.

It's like, please, so you break up with some tenth-grade loser and you get to act like it's the end of the world or something.

Lame.

Super lame. I mean, just because you're in the drama club doesn't mean you have to ACT all the time.

I heard Ms. Archer in the staff room before lunch saying that Katie was an empty vessel waiting to be filled.

Katie IS an empty vessel waiting to be filled.

What do you think that means?

It means she's a slut.

Ms. Archer teaches drama and English and is a freak. She's super skinny and has crazy red hair and is always eating and saying weird stuff like—

I'm telling you, girls. You might think different, but chocolate IS better than sex!

I like her though. I'm a bit of a freak.

Last week in class, Ms. Archer said I have the eyes of a fortune teller. Lisa said that means I wear too much eyeliner.

Dear Diary,

Tonight Lisa's sister Kyla took us to meet her coven.

Lisa put on tons of eyeliner. It looked like her eyes were sinking into deep pools of ink. I had a teeny tiny pentacle on my cheek, but Lisa FREAKED OUT when she saw it.

Are you going to leave that there?

Because, I mean, I just think it would be really embarrassing if one of us was to come off seeming like some high school wannabe.

Right?

You can tell when Lisa's nervous because she acts like I'm an idiot.

Kyla looks like Lisa but she's taller and has boobs.

"I'm really glad you guys are here."

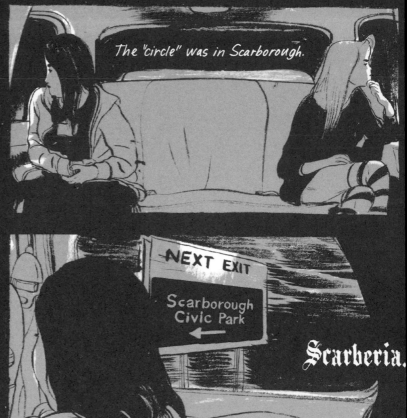

The "circle" was in Scarborough.

NEXT EXIT

Scarborough Civic Park

Scarberia.

So here's the weird thing. Everyone was dressed the SAME! Everyone but us was wearing ugly rock T-shirts and black jeans. Weird.

They looked kind of beat up.

Kyla hugged everyone.

Sarah had a little voice, like a kid.

♪♫ Earth, Air, fire, and Water ♪ Mother Earth I am your daughter All the world so full of spirit There for us if we choose to hear it ♪♫

I don't think Sarah is what most people picture when they talk about witches in the park.

After the song, Manny walked around the circle, touching each of us between the shoulder blades. Then he asked if anyone had anything they wanted to share. And that's when this skinny guy with 80s rocker hair and a turtleneck came forward.

It's funny, because I was so nervous before. I thought, like, wow, witches in the park. Isn't that something people warn you about?

I'd just like to say I love you all and I've been sober for three years now.

Wow.

Amazing.

Blessed be.

Way to go, brother.

I've also been sober for three and a half years. Thanks, everyone.

Altogether six people stepped forward and talked about being sober. Even Kyla.

Kyla also thanked everyone for letting us be there, for helping us on "the path."

Whatever THAT means.

Manny said another long prayer, and the circle was broken, and we all had snacks.

Did you have a good time tonight?

I see the spirit in you.

Yeah. I mean, I thought it was really nice. Really, I mean, really moving. Really spiritual.

It's in here. Beating. Can you feel it?

Just then I had all these thoughts like, "THIS is something else people warn you about," and, "He wants a handjob... or he wants me to kiss him."

It's beating out your future. I can see it.

I see you... in your future, using the spirit. I see...

a woman.

Dear Diary,

JOHN REDDEAR (Katie Matthews' ex-boyfriend) is DEAD!!

He KILLED HIMSELF!!

Lisa said she heard he shot himself!!!

Today, everyone in grade ten got pulled into guidance for a talk with Mrs. Hornet.

Mrs. Hornet smells like baby powder deodorant. She is a very nervous woman.

Mrs. Hornet said she's particularly concerned about people like me, because people like me are prone to depression and depressing stimuli.

Mrs. Hornet says students who are members of the "gothic" culture (i.e. ME) are very fragile.

Truthfully I am always a little depressed but that is just because I am sixteen and everyone is stupid (ha-ha-ha). I doubt it has anything to do with being a goth.

John Reddear was on the VOLLEYBALL TEAM, not a goth, and he KILLED HIMSELF!!!

How come all the girls on the soccer team aren't in counseling?.

Did you hear we're making her a card in phys ed?

Katie Matthews is excused from class because she's suffering from "mental exhaustion."

Everyone has to make her a piece of the card and Julie Peters is going to tape them all together and take them to Katie. It's going to be a "mosaic of mourning."

Barf. Like Katie cares if we make her a card like, "Hi, you don't know me, but I'm sorry your ex-boyfriend is dead."

Did Mrs. Hornet tell you about gothic culture? It's totally discrimination.

I'm a witch and witches don't even believe in suicide.

I believe in suicide but I don't care if John Reddear is dead. I never even KNEW John Reddear.

I think I maybe met him once.

Dear Diary,

Last night Lisa and I tried to summon the spirit of John Reddear, but he didn't appear.

Lisa asked what we would
do if he did show up.

Nothing, I guess. Ignore him.

Yesterday during third period I skipped gym and went down to the ravine.

I try to go to gym, but am forced to skip class whenever balls are involved. I have this thing about balls. Especially airborne balls. Besides, you can't play golf with one arm. So there I was, thinking and stuff, when Ms. Archer walked up.

Well, well, well. A smoker.

CRUNCH CRUNCH

I was just leaving.

Only if you don't have a light on you.

And suddenly I'm talking like there's no tomorrow, which is weird, because I'm not a talker.

It's a rule that if an adult asks to smoke with you, you have to smoke. So we ended up talking and smoking.

I just think it's stupid. I mean, you know, that we're studying all these books... plays... whatever... that everyone studies every year. I mean, they're not even all that interesting, or like, unique. I mean. A LOVE story. No offense.

None taken.

But it's like, why is it so important, that a boy falls in love with a girl? You know, I understand that it's a masterpiece and everything, but there's a part of me that's all like, so what?

When Ms. Archer talks to me, she always looks right into my eyes. Ms. A's eyes are celery green.

Maybe it's more than that. Maybe it's a story of rebellion. Maybe it's a story about two people who fall in love, when falling in love, with the enemy, is the one thing you're not supposed to do. I'm sorry you don't like it.

Oh no. I mean, it's fine. I mean, I'm looking forward to talking about it in class.

You should try that. That talking-in-class thing.

Right.

May I ask you something? Why do the students call you Skim?

Because I'm not.

I see.

I'll assume you prefer Kim.

Sure.

tap tap

Maybe you can try wearing your rebel heart on your sleeve for a while.

27

Three things I will not tell Lisa:

1) My heart feels like a piece of chalk stuck in my throat.

2) I feel like I am definitely a witch, although I am technically only starting to be a witch.

3) I have this piece of paper in my bra.

huff!

Last year, all year, Lisa wore a stone shaped like a heart in her bra as a love charm. When she wore her school shirt sometimes it looked like an extra really big nipple. Lisa didn't think so. But I did.

A Wicca charm can be a thing or a spell or an incantation. It doesn't have to be a rock.

My Wicca book says one spell you can do is cut a piece of paper into a strip and write on it, "My heart will bring my love to me." Three times you write that. Then you tape the two ends of the paper together so it makes a loop.

And that's what I'm wearing in my bra now.

Because of Ms.A

Four things

HEY SKIM!

What?

What are you doing?

Me = stalker

Nothing.

So are you coming to lunch or are you just going to stand there like a freak?

Stand here like a freak.

I'm waiting to talk to Ms. A.

About?

Our papers? Homework?

Stuff.

So talk to her after class.

Need to talk to her now.

Uh. Okay. Weirdo. Do you want me to leave or something?

I thought you said you were going to talk to her?

Right. Well, I just decided I was hungry.

I'm a freak.

You're a spaz.

Fuck you.

Lisa took off after school, so I went home and worked on my altar alone. I sprinkled some glitter over my altar and then realized it looked stupid. It took me an hour and two rolls of tape to get it off again.

Ms. Archer and I have this thing now. When we sit for our talks, Ms. Archer holds my cast.

It's just this thing.

Before Ms. Archer was a teacher at our school, she used to live in a commune with a bunch of artists.

She was a painter and a dancer and she was studying to be a writer.

Ms. Archer says she can't stop looking at my eyes.

She says they are very serious.

This morning over breakfast, Mom asked me about suicide. Because of John Reddear, who is now suddenly part of my life.

I said I am not planning on committing suicide.

Apparently I look unwell. Mom says possibly I am losing weight.

Are you coming to lunch?

Oh. No. I have a meeting.

With Who?

Ms. Archer is helping me with something.

Right.

flush

Did you finish your card yet? For Katie?

I'm not making Katie Matthews a fucking card.

Sssssshhhh

I don't even know Katie Matthews, let alone give a shit about her fucking dead boyfriend, so fuck it.

Wow.

SHAKE

I think it's a total violation. Making little kids try to feel something they don't. I mean, I'm sorry, I just think it's stupid, so I'm not doing the card.

I just made her a little one.

Well, that's you. I'm more independent than you are.

My stomach feels like it's popping, like an ice cube in a warm Pepsi.

Hey. So I was reading my book yesterday. It said witches believe in reincarnation, but it didn't say anything about believing in suicide.

So?

So I was wondering where you read that.

Fuck you. So now you're this all-powerful witch or something, and you know everything about Wicca?

Dear Diary,

Books on Wicca are really long and kind of boring.

I think I know what I'm doing, anyway.

My Wicca book says witches take responsibility for their own actions.

So these are my actions.

They aren't hurting anyone. So be it.

Lisa is not talking to me.

FINE.

Halloween is not actually a witches' holiday.

The actual Wicca festival is called Samhain Lore, which is at the end of summer.

Samhain Lore is a time to communicate with the dead and feast.

Halloween is when a lot of non-witches dress up like witches.

So it's hard to see people as they really are.

Unless they are dressed up like Barbie or Nixon or Freddy, in which case you know they are lame-o freaks.

Both Lisa and I went as witches. We did not discuss this ahead of time, as we are not speaking.

Did you see that Katie Matthews is back? On Halloween. She's dressed as a ballerina. I had this thought, you know, that she might dress up as a ghost.

Unlikely. Did you ever write her a card?

A little one. So, are we talking now?

I don't know. Are you talking to me?

Look. It's just that you were acting really psycho and not really talking about it, so I was just like, what the fuck, you know?

I know.

So what's going on with you and Ms. Archer?

What, I'm some giant lesbo because I'm getting extra help after class?

She acts funny around you.

Whatever. Nothing's happening.

Okay, fine. Are we meeting for gym?

No, I've got something to do.

Fine. Are we meeting after school?

Yes.

>clic.<

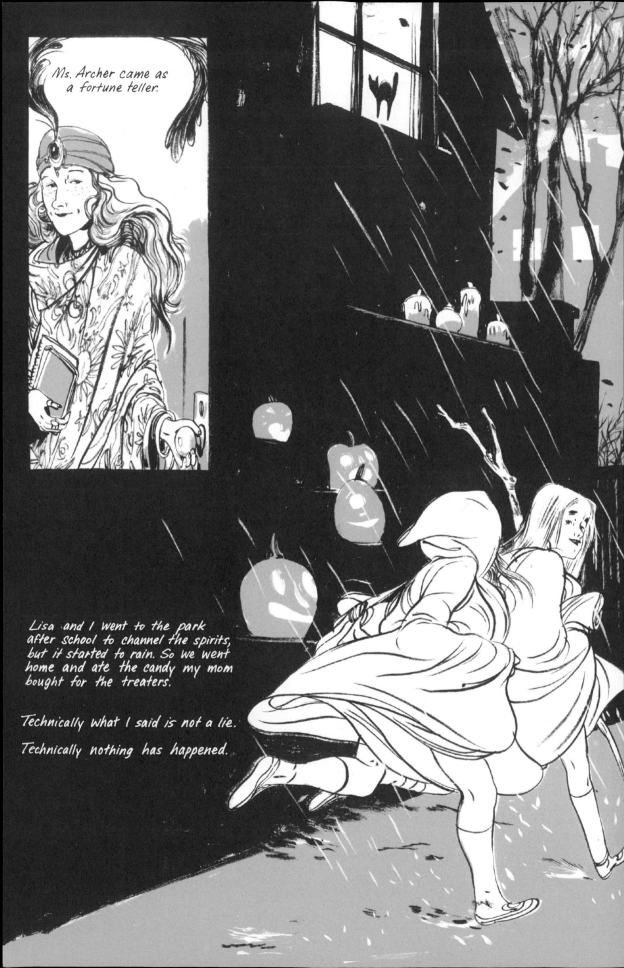

Ms. Archer came as a fortune teller.

Lisa and I went to the park after school to channel the spirits, but it started to rain. So we went home and ate the candy my mom bought for the treaters.

Technically what I said is not a lie.

Technically nothing has happened.

Dear Diary,

For the record, not all Wicca books are boring.
This is what I found in my new book:

The "Charge" comes to each of us in a different
manner. It is that moment in our lives when we
feel the Magick of the Universe coursing through
us for the very first time, and we know beyond
all real and imagined shadows that this calling
to the mysteries is indeed there.

Silver RavenWolf, _To Ride a Silver Broomstick_

Part II
No Rest for the Wicked

Dear Diary,

I had a dream
I put my hands
inside my chest
and held my heart

to try to keep it still

It feels like there's a broken washing machine inside my chest...

or...

a cartoon alarm clock...

Manet, Édouard. Olympia. 1863.

—1862

or...

something...

On Monday Mrs. Hornet announced in prayers that Katie Matthews "accidentally" fell off her roof and broke both her arms.

How do you accidentally fall off a roof?

So I'm like sitting in my room and Julie called me and she was like, Katie's in the hospital.

I know. When I heard, it's like my heart actually stopped beating.

Oh my God.

And it's like, ever since then, I'm totally starving but I can't eat. You know?

Totally. So totally weird.

My school = goldfish tank of stupid.

45

It feels like everyone's so used to being a basket case around here. Like it's becoming like, normal.

This school is totally driving me to smoke.

I know.

Like it's totally okay for someone to cry in biology because the frog they're dissecting makes them think of like, suicide or something...

How is it possible that no one else can hear how loud my heart is beating?

KCHNK

Hey, Skim, what's wrong?

SIP

Nothing.

Something.

Maybe nothing.

Something...

46

ear Diary,

s. Archer wasn't in class
day. Mrs. Hornet came in
d told us to read quietly.

Mrs. Hornet?

Does this mean our Shakespeare test is canceled?

I have no idea, dear. But I would assume not.

Do you know when we would know if it was canceled?

Hey, maybe it's catching.

Maybe Ms. A jumped off a roof!

Dear Diary,

When I was six I was in the school play and they ran out of parts for people. And so I was the Night Sky.

And my dad was like, "But there is no knight in Our Town."

CRUNCH

CRUNCH

Mom said I should tell people I was the moon.

P.S.

Mom is NOT a light sleeper.

Good thing I'm not a drug addict or anything or I could easily rob her blind.

Dear Diary,

Today in prayers Julie Peters (Katie M's best friend) announced that she is starting a new club.

The
G (irls)
C (elebrate)
L (ife) club

Oh fucking BRU-THER.

Julie Peters is a BIG IDIOT COW!

giggle giggle

hee!

Ha-ha! Doesn't some kid die at the end of that movie?

Yeah.

I can't believe it's the GIRLS celebrate life and there's a picture of a dead guy on their board AND they're watching a dead guy movie.

Maybe we should have gone to some photography club meetings.

Do you think this is a club for people who are going to commit suicide or people who know people who might commit suicide?

Why, are you thinking of joining?

Ha! I'd rather hang myself!

Shoot yourself in the head!

Eat rat poison!!!

Slit your wrists!

Jump off a roof!

Dive in front of a bus!

SNORT! HA!

HA! HA!

HA! HA!

HA

HA

brrrijjinngg!!!!!

I am just going over to drop off this drawing.

Then I'm going home and going to bed.

It's funny. I don't remember telling you where I lived.

I know. I'm sorry.

Don't be sorry. Is that for me?

Dear Diary,

This weekend I studied my Shakespeare and read my fortune a million times.

Five times I got The Lovers as my "self" card.

The Lovers

The Lovers = love and relationships, new beginnings, new connections.

The Angel on the card = FATE. Fate is the force that makes you do things and choose things that you don't always understand. Destiny.

BUT... if you get this card reversed = upside down...

...it means a bad decision, an untrustworthy person, a state of imbalance.

The last time I did my fortune, I got The Lovers reversed.

Possible reasons:

• I have an untrustworthy person in my life (?Lisa?)

• I did my fortune too many times (and therefore last time doesn't count)

Dear Diary,

Today in prayers we sang "Oh Happy Day."

In spare the whole grade ten had to go to the music portable and do "self-love" exercises with Mrs. Hornet and this woman who's from an institute for teenage problems or something.

Lisa says self-love is another word for masturbation.

The woman had huge bug eyes and kept trying to make eye contact with everyone, like a crazy person or a serial killer.

We had to write down the things that make us sad and share it with the class, if we felt comfortable. People wrote: Suicide, Illness, Death and Loss.

One girl said that Unhappiness made her sad.

IGNORANCE

Then we had to write what makes us happy.

I didn't know what to write.

Because...

I'm not sure.

I didn't know what other people would think about my answer.

It's a stupid question.

I didn't feel like sharing my list but after class Mrs. Hornet asked if she could see it.

So much for feeling comfortable.

On my way to my locker Julie Peters came up and gave me an invitation to come watch Dead Poets Society.

What did you write?

My family.

Your family makes you happy?

It's clearly a meaningless exercise of school paranoia, so whatever.

Clearly.

flic

So do you want to come over and rent a movie later?

I have this thing I have to do tonight... with my dad.

Oh. Okay.

Later.

I can't believe Lisa said her family makes her happy.

Lisa is full of crap.

Dear Diary,

There are girls at my school who think people are in love with them all the time, like Marty Spencer who is crazy rich and owns two horses and is always being "loved on" by men. Men like:

- the security guard with the lazy eye

- the art teacher

- her riding instructor

- her boyfriend's best friend

I am so loved on right now, you guys. It's so totally crazy.

It's hard to tell if love makes people feel better or worse. I think it makes Marty feel better.

Lisa has never been in love and doesn't believe in love.

Neither does my mother.

My parents fell out of love the year my mother got a job at WRE Publicity. Mom found her job more fulfilling than her marriage.

Mom said love is no paycheck.

My dad still believes in love...

That's the story of love, baby!

Right now he's dating a woman who makes mugs. I get a new mug every month.

You can put your potions in it.

Thanks.

Any teen drama I should know about? Any boyfriends?

No.

Every time I see my dad he says...

You know you can talk to me about anything, right?

I think I'm in love

Kim?

I'm okay. I'm just... full.

Being in love is not what I expected.

Dear Diary,

When I got home from dinner I called Ms. A on the phone but no one answered so I hung up. I'm not sure if I'm supposed to do that.

I put her number under my altar.

Things That Make Me Sad

Love

Things That Make Me Happy

Love?

Dear Diary,

Katie Matthews is back (again). Both her arms are in casts and her right ankle is all wrapped up. And her face looks all ~~funny~~ wrinkly. A bunch of students followed her around all day carrying her things.

I bet she's on tons of anti-depressants.

Katie looks like the Grim Reaper.

Dear Diary,

Ms. Archer was busy today and I only saw her in class.

clic...

clic...

~~She didn't really look at me.~~

* My Shakespeare-inspired Thought for the Day:

When you read Romeo and Juliet it doesn't talk a lot about how Juliet was feeling when she knew she was in love with Romeo and wasn't supposed to be. Considering the ending, there's not a lot of that in there.

I wonder if Shakespeare wrote a draft that had Juliet being so nervous she had really bad cramps and had to pee all the time.

Hey, you know what I was thinking today in class?

What?

That Katie Matthews and John Reddear are like Romeo and Juliet,

on a delay...

And Katie didn't die.

Right... Hey, so...

Everything Lisa says drives me crazy these days.

I should tell her that. She would freak out though.

If Juliet could have just suffered in silence and got married and pretended everything was okay and not said anything, maybe things would have turned out better.

What?

Nothing.

P.S. Today I dropped my papier mâché head in art class and everyone laughed. Thus confirming my suspicion that despite all this touchy-feely stuff, the girls at my school are still jerks.

Dear Diary,

Last night I went to Ms. Archer's house again. I don't know if she expected to see me.

She seemed distracted, kind of nervous. She said she was looking for something.

I was only there for a little while when the phone rang and she left me downstairs by myself. She said she only has one phone because she hates the phone.

But she was up there for a while.

All over her house things were in piles. There were books all over the floor.

In her hall there is a picture of Ms. Archer when she was a teenager. She is standing in the ocean with a man that looks like her dad. It is the only photograph in the whole house.

I looked at it for a long time.

I put my tarot cards on her table for her to find later.

Today in gym we did anti-stress breathing relaxation exercises and I fell asleep on my mat.

Dear Diary,

Today I stayed very still on the couch all day.

I am trying not to be obsessive. It is not good to only think about one ~~person~~ thing.

But at the same time...

It is hard not to think about something.

Yesterday Ms. Archer told me I shouldn't come over to her house for a while. She said ,she will see me at school...

KIM, IS THIS YOUR MESS IN HERE?!

which is fine and no big deal.

Dear Diary,

Someone wrote DEATH IS COOL! on the GCL board this morning.

The GCL got permission to fix it during spare. They were freaking out about it all day.

You know, in some schools they send you to jail for this sort of thing.

In history I could feel a million angry GCL eyes drilling into my back.

Oooooh! So we shouldn't touch the board because it's SCHOOL PROPERTY. Woo.

Everyone thinks I did it.

Whatever, Julie totally thinks I did it. She gave me an ugly look at recess. Like I'm scared of Julie Peters. What's she going to do? Get her mother to run me over with her minivan?

Ha-ha.

Maybe if you lightened up, people wouldn't think you were looking to off yourself.

What do you mean?

Look, whatever. It's no big deal. Chill out.

I am chill.

Lisa should shut up.

Dear Diary,

I woke up this morning and my mouth tasted like ice cream from a paper cup.

I had this dream I had this little yellow bear as a pet and I kept it in one of my dad's stupid girlfriend mugs.

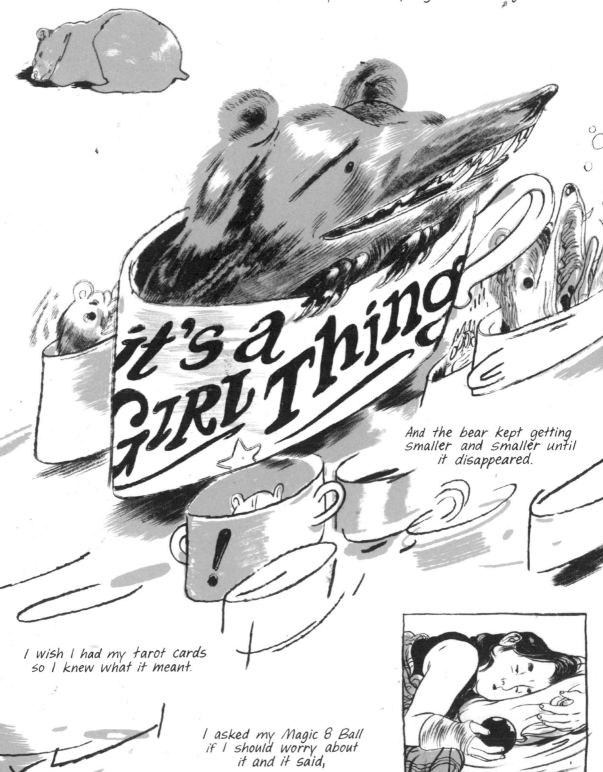

it's a GIRL Thing

And the bear kept getting smaller and smaller until it disappeared.

I wish I had my tarot cards so I knew what it meant.

I asked my Magic 8 Ball if I should worry about it and it said,

"Without a doubt."

Magic 8 Balls suck.

Dear Diary,

Today in prayers I was singing (sort of) "Joyful, Joyful," and I got a sick feeling.

Ms. Archer is leaving.

She is going to some art thing in New Mexico and so she will not be finishing the year with us. Mrs. Hornet will finish the section.

Yeah. So maybe it won't be so bad. We can torture The Hornet. We can come to class with blood dripping from our fangs. Or our wrists! We can be suicidal goths. She'll have a nervous breakdown trying to stop us from killing ourselves.

Yeah.

toss

That sucks, I guess.

Yes.

yeah. Did you know she was leaving?

I don't understand.

No.

That's weird.

Why didn't she tell me?

SHITHEAD!!

Are you okay? You look funny.

I'm fine, okay? Just drop it.

SNAP!

I left school early.

At the bus station I ran into one of the witches from Kyla's circle.

Hey, you! I know you. You okay?

Yes.

Hey, are you still goin' to the circle?

Oh. No.

It was a good space, eh? Unfortunately I had to leave because, uh, too many people were hooking up. That's not healthy.

Hey, if you and your friend are ever interested, I started a magazine for Wiccans. The Other Faith. We're always looking for interviews and models. Free copy for you.

the Other Faith

Thanks.

Cheer up, kid. Remember, the spirits work in mysterious ways.

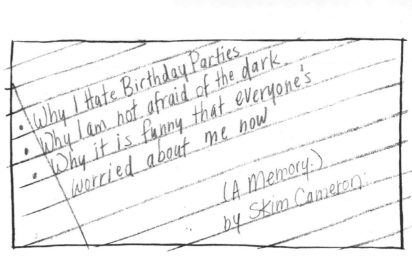

- Why I Hate Birthday Parties.
- Why I am not afraid of the dark.
- Why it is funny that everyone's worried about me now

(A Memory.)
by Skim Cameron.

The last birthday party I went to was Julie Peters' thirteenth birthday in grade seven. It was a costume party.

I went as the Cowardly Lion from the Wizard of Oz.

Everyone at the party was a ballerina or a figure skater.

Hey, are you a bear?

Hey, everyone, Skim's a bear!

I'm Elizabeth Manley.

Oh my God! I loved her!

The only other non-figure skater was Hien Warshowski, who came dressed as a soldier.

Julie Peters was a prima ballerina and she had real toe shoes with ribbons.

I think maybe Julie's mom made her invite us. I only got my invitation the day before the party.

Okay, girls, I'm going up to listen to my tapes. Call me if you need anything. Don't eat too much junk.

All night Julie and her friends talked about their country club and this guy who worked there who had blue eyes and looked like Don Johnson.

DEVON!!!

Oh my God! I want to kiss him!

Oh my God me too!

Hien and I watched The Secret of NIMH in the living room.

Until about half way into the night when suddenly we heard...

AIR RAID!!

AIR RAID!!!

And then this herd of ballerinas swooped into the room and chased Hien and me out of the house.

Why are you eating cookies? Didn't you just have cake?

I'm still hungry.

Did Julie like her present?

Sure.

Have an apple. There are apples in the fridge.

I told my mom the party ended early.

Okay. I'm just going to sit outside.

And do what?

On Monday, Julie left a note on my desk thanking me for the U2 tape I got her.

Hien moved to Sudbury the next year.

Dear Diary,

I HATE EVERYTHIN

It's Snowing.

Part III
Goodbye (Hello)

Dear Diary,

Today instead of phys ed we had a memorial ceremony on the upper athletic field, which is almost frozen.

All the grade ten girls released white balloons with messages of hope for all victims of suicide/peer pressure/depression

=people who died and all the people they left behind.

It wasn't just for the victims of suicide, because Mrs. Hornet says we are not here to focus on the negative (dead people).

(John)

John Reddear's parents and Katie's parents were there. And some boys from the volleyball team.

(But not Katie.)

The CBC was there too.

On the six o'clock news you could hear Julie Peters saying, "It's not about dwelling on past tragedy. It's about celebrating the living spirit."

This is the stuff that I have heard about John since he died.

1) That he was happy, outgoing and athletic, and he liked volleyball and music.

2) That he was secretly suffering from depression.

3) That he was MAYBE a star volleyball player and depressed person who was ALSO in love with a boy who was on the St. Michael's second-string volleyball team.

Maybe this is why he decided to overdose on his mother's heart pills (Note: Lisa said she never said he shot himself. It was just a RUMOR.)

No one talked about John being gay at the ceremony.

Surprise, surprise.

Although Julie Peters practically ripped Anna Cunard's tongue out when she brought it up afterwards.

P.S. No one knows if the boy from the volleyball team loved John back...

Hey, look. She WAS at school today.

Special treatment. Of course.

Well. I mean, she's still pretty upset. I guess you never get over something like that.

Whatever. She's totally karmically and mentally screwed now.

What do you mean by that?

Well, if you think about it, no matter what happens now, her life is totally fucked.

I mean, so okay, so she graduates from high school. And she goes to Queen's or somewhere in the States...

NYU.

No. I'm going to NYU. She can go to Arizona.

Because you can't go to the same university?

Listen! Okay, so at university she meets this perfect boy who plays on the golf team. Bret Ready.

Bret Ready?

CLIC CLIC

TEEN Spirit

And they're all happy and they date for four years and then they get married in the Bahamas. Or Toronto.

Not Arizona?

Whatever. And it's SOOOO perfect. It ends up in the newspaper because it's SOOOO perfect.

APPLY

Uh-huh.

And they have two kids —two girls— and they have a big house and a cottage and a minivan and a Corvette and they go to a fancy golf club and...

AND...

Okay, can I get to my point? My POINT is that even like, twenty years from now, she'll be sitting in her perfect golf club eating a club sandwich with no-fat mayo and her fancy husband who has no soul and is balding, and EVEN THEN she will still be the girl whose boyfriend committed suicide because he was a fag.

So?

So I'm just saying ... she will be scarred for life, that's all. Because of this, after now, her life will never be perfect.

Oh.

I didn't know it was for sure that he was gay.

It is.

SLAM

Oh.

Where are you going?

For a smoke.

I thought you were coming to the library...

I'll see you in spare.

Dear Diary,

I don't necessarily mean to be avoiding Lisa but I am.

We were supposed to eat in the caf but instead I went to the Swiss Chalet by myself.

Swiss Chalet = Social black hole.

It's full of old people with no teeth and bad lungs who eat French fries and cough and get mad if you make too much noise. Over the booths all you can see are little clumps of curly white hair. Like little poodle heads.

On the speakers they play Barry Manilow and ABBA without the singing.

pat pat

When I was leaving I saw the GCL coming out of the 7-Eleven with Diet Cokes and Doritos.

Katie was at the back. Her face looked like a bag of stones, hard and small.

Hey, where were you?

Lunch.

Oh. Well. Ms. Archer was here getting her stuff from her office. You just missed her.

Just now?!

Like two minutes ago.

Dear Diary,

All day today I was rubber.
My eyes felt like bathtub plugs.

I tried to take up as little
space as possible.

Everyone is watching me

Julie   Lisa

Mrs. Hornet   Mom

I do not give
two craps though.

GRIND
GRIND

When I got home I ate
three frozen yogurt bars,
a bag of peanuts and some
cheese and went to bed.

All the spells for bringing someone back to you need hair from the person who has left.

How are you supposed to get hair if the person ~~won't talk to you~~ is gone?

Witchcraft = total crap.

You are never really alone
in the city at night.

There are always

taxi drivers
coffee shop people
the 7-Eleven guy
people in their homes
watching talk shows

It just feels lonely.

Dear Diary,

Today we had swimming in phys ed. Mrs. Henry sent Katie and me to pick up photocopies from the office. Julie Peters offered to help but Mrs. Henry said the task was for "cast-offs" only.

Gym teachers are so cool!

So.

I realized I don't think I have ever talked to Katie Matthews. Ever.

SNAP!

So.

Is it itchy?

Sort of. The big one is itchy.

I'm kind of dreading getting rid of it and having to do gym.

I guess.

Who drew the heart on your cast?

Ms. Archer.

When I say her name it feels like a candy that accidentally slipped out of my mouth.

It's too bad she's leaving.

It is.

So is it true you're a witch?

Well, I mean, Lisa and I... I'm working on it.

I'm almost a witch.

I like your star.

Thanks. It's a pentacle. It's supposed to protect me.

From what?

Everything, I guess. Probably not bullets or anything.

Huh.

It's mostly just symbolic.

Can we stop a minute? I'm not ready to go back.

You have a lot of daisies on your casts.

I know.

Katie looked at the daisies on her cast like they were spiders. Like she wanted to crush them.

I looked for Lisa after school, but someone said she saw her leave with Anna Canard. If she joins the GCL I will laugh SO HARD.

I saw this movie on TV about this woman who was in mourning because her whole family died and she cut off all her hair. I thought of doing that but then I thought maybe I'm not skinny enough. And then I would look crazy instead of mournful.

I'm coming in there in five minutes to watch Sisters!

Not that I necessarily want to look mournful... or crazy.

P.S. The only time my mother cries is when she is watching Sisters. That is totally bizarre.

Dear Diary,

SNIP!

Before anyone goes around talking about how I am acting weird they should consider the recent changes THEY have decided to make in THEIR social lives.

KIIIIIMMMM! Please pick up the PHONE!

Hey.

Hello. Skim. So. I wanted to ask you something. If I got us dates for the dance, would you go?

Are you serious?

Yes.

Why?

Dear Diary,

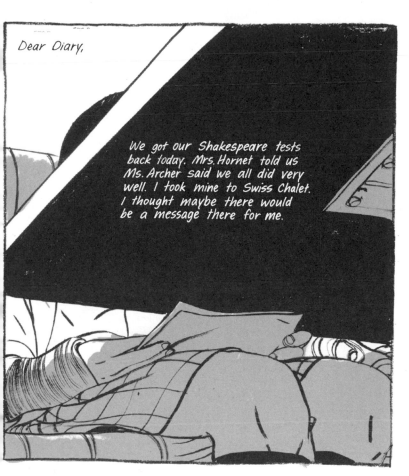

We got our Shakespeare tests back today. Mrs. Hornet told us Ms. Archer said we all did very well. I took mine to Swiss Chalet. I thought maybe there would be a message there for me.

Something.

When Ms. Archer marks, her pencil barely touches the paper. All you see are ghostly little checks and x's. At the end of the paper she wrote:

Kim,
I'm glad to see you have developed an appreciation for Romeo and Juliet, as your work here clearly demonstrates.
Excellent work.

Ms. Archer.

Hey, Skim!

Hey.

Are you going for lunch?

I just got lunch.

Oh.

So can I ask you a stupid question?

Yeah.

Can you open my gum for me?

There are only a couple of things you can do with one hand. Katie says sometimes it makes her feel like doing nothing forever, until she gets hungry.

Dear Diary,

I have no idea what is going on in any of my classes.

NAME THE STATE.

Biology = complete blank

American history = no idea

Art = papier mâché only
= Okay

Chemistry = a blur

Math 10 = no clue

I'm like an alien every time I sit at my desk. I don't even know if I'm supposed to have a protractor for math.

I don't even have any notes for most of my classes, only drawings.

Great. Me = seriously screwed.

English = Okay

Lisa was all giddy today because last night she and Anna Canard went to John Reddear's house to search his garbage for gay porn and other mementos.

Anna Canard has a face like a guinea pig.

Did you find anything?

Lisa is always trying to stare me down.

No. It wasn't garbage day so we just looked in their windows.

That's kind of weird.

Why?

I don't know. What will you do if you find something?

Well, Kyla said it's easier to contact a spirit if you have something that connects them to the living world. I thought we were still trying to contact his spirit.

121

Today I went to the hospital and the doctor sawed my cast off.

My arm looks like a dead rat.

The doctor threw the cast out but I fished it out of the garbage and put it in my bag.

It's a bit smelly.

SNIFF SNIFF

At school everyone is freaking out about the dance.

There are all these useless posters up even though everyone already knows about it.

Even Katie is going, although I'm pretty sure she doesn't want to.

Mom bought me a red dress. It's velvet and heavy on the cleavage so she got me a shawl too.

Ricky called and said he couldn't get his dad's car so we would have to meet them at the school.

Car-less geeks.

Dear Diary,

I think there are a lot of ways to be marked.

If you are ugly, like Natasha Cake who has no eyebrows and doesn't wash her hair, then you are marked to be treated like crap for life.

I have eyebrows and wash but I think I am also marked to some degree (biologically) as a weirdo for life. (Mom says that there is nothing about my appearance that I don't contribute to with my habits.)

People can also mark you. Scott Bouffant marked me in grade nine with a disgusting hickey that didn't go away for a week.

Me = slut for a whole week.

(He never even called me afterwards because I wouldn't give him a handjob— BECAUSE I'D JUST MET HIM!!!)

Lisa's mother got drunk once and told us that all relationships leave a scar. Lisa said her mother was talking about VD (=Venereal Disease — I had to look it up). Lisa said you could have a VD and not even know it.

I think everything you do and everything people do to you leaves a mark, or at least it affects who you are.

Today when we were sitting out of gym (my arm is still sore), Katie told me the doctor said her left shoulder might need an operation. Katie grits her teeth when she talks. I don't know if she used to. Every time she scrapes her teeth together it looks like she's getting ready for a fall or a jump.

I wonder if when the casts are gone, she'll still do that.

Dear Diary,

When people in the movies talk about tarot cards, they always talk about the Death card and say it doesn't necessarily mean you're going to die.

It's change.

But almost all the cards = change.

This is the thing about school dances. They make like it's supposed to be this other-worldly thing, but really it's just the people you see every day dressed up, standing in the gym in the dark with Red Hot Chili Peppers playing.

Lisa stood next to me for three songs. Then she disappeared with this guy.

I think the gym was supposed to look like heaven.

This one song came on and everyone ran onto the dance floor and started dancing with their arms over their heads, waving at the ceiling. It's amazing how, when you don't feel something everyone else feels, it just looks like nothing. Like watching people dance to a song you don't like.

Katie smiles the smallest smiles on the planet.

Where are you going?

We're leaving. Kim and I are leaving.

To go where?

Out.

Skim. I would really appreciate it if you would let me have this conversation privately with Katie and stay out of it.

I just realized today that Julie Peters thinks she is a mom.

Look. I don't feel like being here. I TOLD you I didn't want to come. You said I had to. I did. And NOW I'm leaving.

Okay, Katie, but I have to say that I'm totally disgusted that you don't seem to care at ALL that all of this was done for YOU and you're just stepping all over all your friends' efforts.

What are you talking about?

I'm TALKING about this dance, which just happens to be a FUNDRAISER for a service that would have saved your boyfriend's LIFE.

You keep calling him my boyfriend but he broke up with me.

He was under emotional stress! If John had had a proper support system none of this would have happened.

You don't know that.

What?

How could you know that?

Oh, and you know better?

NO. I'm just saying only a crazy person would say she could see into the mind of a dead boy. You're not a psychic. You're a high school student.

I realize this contradicts my intentions to channel John's spirit but a) Julie doesn't know we were going to do that and b) Julie Peters would never channel anyone's spirit.

She's just a know-it-all pain in the butt.

I'm sorry I said that about John. I'm sorry I called him a dead boy.

Well... he is.

They're totally going to know we wrecked the GCL board.

I wrecked it.

Right.

I don't care.

Katie stood very still for a long time after she said that. Snow kept falling and sticking to her hair.

Do you want to get a coffee or something? Or like, a tea?

Mistake?

Sure.

Dear Diary,

Katie is always over here now. She says my house is much calmer than her house. Katie says her mother is kind of a wreck. My house is practically deserted so I guess it seems calm.

Katie is obsessed with British people and British comedies. After we study we watch Monty Python videos.

Katie = a bit of a weirdo!

Lisa is always going to St. John's Collegiate with Anna to visit this boy she met at the dance. So I almost never see her. When I do see her she is wearing lip gloss and scarves. She looks like that girl from Grease.

Katie said Anna Canard is obsessed with boys and is a huge slut. Katie said that Anna always has cold sores because she has herpes (which some boy at canoe camp gave her). I wonder if Lisa knows.

Probably not.

The GCL are all holy and religious now that they are organizing the school Christmas play.

Julie Peters is currently channeling the Virgin Mary in prep for the big show.

I moved my altar to my dresser. I put all my old spells in a jar with Ms. Archer's phone number and some other things. It's under my bed.

I'm too screwed for school to be a witch right now.

Dear Diary,

Lisa looks different.

All day today she walked around school carrying this gigantic black sweater that has big holes in the sleeves.

It's SAM'S sweater.

Sam= Lisa's new boyfriend.
Lisa said Sam is fiercely independent.

It's a rare thing, you know, the ability to think independently. More people should try it.

As soon as school was over she put on the sweater and we had a smoke to catch up.

I so don't have any time for that. I mean, I sort of feel like I can't study right now, you know? I feel like I have to live a little right now...

Sure, why not?

So what are you up to?

Studying.

Being in love changes you, you know?

Yeah.

I can't explain it, obviously. I mean, it's very complex. No one can put it in words.

No.

It's just... it makes things different, you know? It's like, you turn a corner.

Yeah, I can see that.

It's kind of amazing.

It is.

Well, I'm going to meet Sam.

tug tug

Okay, later.

ACKNOWLEDGMENTS

Jillian and Mariko thank (in order of appearance): Emily Pohl-Weary (who first published Part I of Skim for the comic series Kiss Machine Presents...), agent extraordinaire Sam Hiyate, and Patsy Aldana, Shelley Tanaka, Michael Solomon and everyone at Groundwood Books for all their support.